Planet Pee Wee

Planet Pee Wee

Judy Delton

Illustrated by Alan Tiegreen

A Yearling Book

Published by
Bantam Doubleday Dell Books for Young Readers
a division of
Bantam Doubleday Dell Publishing Group, Inc.
1540 Broadway
New York, New York 10036

Visit us on the Web! www.bdd.com
Educators and librarians, visit the BDD Teacher's Resource Center at www.bdd.com/teachers

ISBN: 0-440-41333-8

Printed in the United States of America

May 1998

10 9 8 7 6 5 4 3 2 1

CWO

For New Baby, Grace, who isn't a new baby
anymore, with love
from Grandma Mama

Contents

CHAPTER 1

Mud Slide

"Look out ahead!" shouted Roger White, tearing past the other Pee Wee Scouts on his bike.

It was too late. His bike skidded in the mud, throwing big black splashes onto Rachel Meyers.

"Roger White, this is my new jacket, and it says 'dry clean only'!" shouted Rachel. "It has silk in it! You're going to pay for this!"

Roger's bike was stuck in a big, squishy mud rut. Rachel walked up and gave it a shove. Over toppled Roger into the rut. He sank deeper and deeper. The more he tried to get out, the more the mud squished up between his arms and legs and fingers. It's not easy to stand up when mud is pulling you down.

"You shouldn't try to get back at Roger," said Molly Duff to Rachel. "He's mean."

"Pooh," said Rachel, brushing off her jacket. The more she brushed, the worse the mud looked. "I'm not afraid of him."

Molly looked at Roger. He didn't seem mad at all. He was laughing.

"Hey, look at me," he called. "I'm taking a mud bath!"

Roger pretended to wash himself with an imaginary bar of soap. He rubbed it on his neck and under his arms.

"You look like one of those mud wrestlers on TV!" shouted Kevin Moe. "That looks like fun."

"It is," said Roger, sliding over on his stomach.

The other boys looked as if they wanted to try taking a mud bath but were not quite brave enough.

"Come on in, the water's great," called Roger. He grabbed Kevin's shoe. Kevin grabbed Tim Noon's arm, and both boys tumbled into the mud with Roger.

"What's your mom going to say when they come to the Pee Wee meeting all covered with mud?" said Mary Beth Kelly to Molly. "They can't go to your house like that!"

It was Tuesday. Tuesday was Pee Wee Scouts meeting day. Molly's mother, Mrs. Duff, was their temporary leader while Mrs. Peters was out of town. Molly knew her mother would not welcome mud-covered Pee Wees on her clean floors and flowered sofa. Molly thought of mud on the table and chairs and even on their treat of chocolate cupcakes. Rat's knees, things looked bad.

"It's the January thaw," said Tracy Barnes. "This happens every year. My mom hates it."

"I like it. It feels like spring is coming," said Patty Baker, who was Kenny's twin sister. They were both Pee Wee Scouts.

"Spring is a long way off, dummy," said Sonny Stone. "I don't see any grass or flowers around here."

Now everyone was getting wild, thought Molly. Kenny Baker was sliding in the mud. And Lisa Ronning was making mud castles as if she were at the beach.

"You guys are crazy," said Rachel, stamping her foot. "I'll bet Mrs. Duff cancels our meeting!"

A mud fight began, and Jody George's wheelchair got stuck in the middle of it.

"It's not like Jody to get in trouble," said Mary Beth.

"It was an accident," said Molly. "He got stuck in that rut."

Before long a neighbor's dog came running by and jumped on Roger. Then the dog turned into a mud dog.

Soon there was not one clean Pee Wee in the crowd.

"What are we going to do?" asked Tracy. "We can't go to Scouts like this."

"I know," said Kevin, who was a good problem solver. Molly liked Kevin almost as much as she liked Jody. She wanted to marry one of them someday.

"We can roll in the snow and get clean!" Kevin said.

"Yeah!" shouted Sonny, throwing himself from the muddy rut into a snowbank.

All the Pee Wees followed. But the snow was wet. That was what happened in a January thaw.

"We still have mud on us, but now it's dripping," groaned Rachel.

Lisa wiped her face with a muddy mitten. Now her face was muddy too.

"Yuck," said Mary Beth. "Your mom is going to kill us!"

CHAPTER 2

Take Me to Your Leader

When the scouts got to Molly's house, it was not Mrs. Duff who opened the door. It was Mrs. Peters!

"Surprise!" she said. "I'm back!"

When she saw the muddy Pee Wees, her smile turned to a frown. "Why, look at you! You all look like candy bars dipped in milk chocolate!"

"Surprise!" said Roger. "We fell in a mud bath."

"Candy bars!" yelled Sonny. "Gobble

9

gobble gobble, I'm going to eat everyone up!"

Soon most of the Pee Wees were pretending to be candy bars.

Mrs. Peters and Mrs. Duff did not look pleased to have chocolate-covered Scouts.

They helped everyone strip off the muddy clothes, and the Pee Wees took turns at the laundry tub in the basement washing up. Mrs. Duff put the jackets that did not say "dry clean only" into the washer.

"Now," said Mrs. Duff. "Half of our meeting time is over already!"

"It's Roger's fault," said Rachel.

Mrs. Peters held up her hand before an argument could begin about whose fault the mud was.

"I just got back today," she said, "but I had to come right over because I missed you all so much."

The Pee Wees cheered. Molly didn't mind her mother's helping out, but it was never as much fun when your own mom was in charge. Mrs. Peters would turn everything back to normal. The meetings would be in her basement again, where there was lots of room for games and projects.

"While I was gone," said Mrs. Peters, "I gave a lot of thought to our new badge. I think it's one you'll all like and have fun working on."

"Is it a badge for being muddy?" asked Tim.

Rachel groaned. "Anyone can get muddy," she sighed. "You don't get a badge for doing that. What is the real badge, Mrs. Peters?"

"Well," said their leader, "when I was out of town I met someone who is an astronaut."

Here the Pee Wees interrupted her again.

"Yay! We're all going to the moon!" shouted Roger. "When do we leave?"

"I don't want to go to the moon," cried

Sonny. "I'm afraid of heights. It's an allergy."

"Fear of heights is a phobia," said Mary Beth. "Not an allergy."

"Well, the moon is too high, anyway," said Sonny.

"We are not going to the moon," said Mrs. Peters. "But the astronaut I met will come and talk to us, and we can read all about space in books in the library. Then I thought we would go to the planetarium. They have a model of the whole galaxy there, and we can feel as if we're right up close to the stars and planets."

The Pee Wees cheered. This space badge sounded exciting. Sonny was the only one who was worried.

"I think we should really go to the moon," said Roger. "We could have our own spaceship with 'Pee Wees' written on the side of it. And we could go to other planets and make new friends."

12

"Like, you know, a matador," said Tim.

"A matador is a bullfighter," said Kevin. "You mean a meteor."

"A meteor is part of a star or something," said Kenny.

"I think Tim means an ambassador," said Jody, who was very smart and knew a lot of hard words. "An ambassador goes to foreign countries to spead goodwill."

"That's it!" said Tim. "Can we do that, Mrs. Peters? Can we go and spread goodwill, please?"

Mrs. Peters and Mrs. Duff were smiling. "I doubt that we can go to the moon," said Molly's mother. "But we can learn about space and spacecraft and planets and stars and have a good time doing it. And when we have each done a project of our own that has to do with space, we'll get our space badge."

Now all the Pee Wees cheered, even Sonny.

"And I have even more news," said their leader. "The Pee Wee Scout officials in Washington have decided to sponsor a contest. They will choose one Pee Wee from each troop across the nation to go to Camp Blast Off next summer. The person with the best project will win. A judge will come to look at your projects when you're finished with them. Then they'll choose the winner. So one of you, or two if you're working together, will go to camp and meet Pee Wees from all over the world. You'll live like a real astronaut for one whole week. You'll eat space food and wear a space suit and see how it feels to float in space. I hear the space capsule you'll go in is the real thing. And you'll take a moon walk that you'll never forget. Our visiting astronaut will tell us more about Camp Blast Off."

Now the Pee Wees were clapping and shouting.

"I want all of you to think very hard

about one special project you can do to try to win the contest and earn this badge. You could draw a picture of a spacecraft, or make up a recipe for space food, or report on the planets. You could write a play about children living on Mars, or even build a little make-believe galaxy out of clay.

"Today I brought with me some pictures of Saturn, Mars, and Venus to color. Just look at all the rings around Saturn! Those rings are made of ice and rock. If we color three planets a week, we'll have a fine collection of all the planets when we're through!"

"I've got a book about the planets at home," said Kevin. "Maybe I'll bring it to our next meeting."

"I'm sure none of you has ever met a real astronaut," said Mrs. Peters. "So that's another very exciting thing about this badge."

"Boy, this is great!" said Rachel to Molly.

16

"A real astronaut, and a contest, and a badge!"

Molly nodded. Now all she had to do was think of the very best project in the world! There was more than a badge at stake this time. This could be her ticket to Camp Blast Off! What could she do to make sure *she* was the one to walk on that moon?

CHAPTER 3

Top Secret

After the meeting, the Pee Wees put on their semiclean jackets and started walking home. All except Molly and Mary Beth, who sat on Molly's front steps to talk.

"I can't wait to go to Camp Blast Off," said Roger as he passed them.

"Ho ho ho," said Mary Beth. "You aren't going to Camp Blast Off, we are!"

Roger snorted. "What do girls know about space?" he said. "Only guys can be astronauts."

"That's a lie," said Molly. "Girls can be anything boys can be."

"No way," said Roger. "Girls would be wimpy astronauts. Did you ever see an astronaut wearing gooky makeup, or a dress? I say Sonny and I will win that trip, hands down."

"Liar, liar, pants on fire," said Mary Beth. "You just wait and see, Mr. Know-it-all."

But Roger had covered his ears and was running down the street, laughing.

"Do you think he's right about girls not making good astronauts?" Mary Beth asked Molly.

"Of course not," said Molly. "He's so dumb."

"Well, our project will have to be really, really good," said Mary Beth.

Molly noticed Mary Beth had said "our project." She asked, "Are we doing one together?"

"Of course," said Mary Beth. "We're best friends. And it will take both of us to come up with something to beat Roger."

"What about Jody and Kevin and Rachel?" said Molly. "They always have really good projects."

"Well, ours is going to have to be better," said Mary Beth, sighing. "We're going to have to come up with something really great."

The girls thought some more.

"I know what the best thing of all would be," said Molly. "It would be to build a real rocket and really go to the moon. Boy, would Roger and Mrs. Peters ever be surprised."

"How could we do that?" asked Mary Beth.

"I don't know, but I know no one else could beat us. We'd be sure to win the contest."

Just saying the words made Molly quiver with excitement. Could they build their own rocket? If they worked really hard, could they go to the moon?

Or was Molly's wild imagination running away with her again?

"Where would we get our own rocket?" asked Mary Beth. "They don't sell them at the mall."

"We'd have to build it," said Molly. "I'll bet we could."

"Wow," said Mary Beth. "Wouldn't Mrs. Peters be surprised if we built our own rocket? We'd get our badge just like that!" She snapped her fingers. "We wouldn't have to draw pictures or make up recipes for space food or write reports. We wouldn't have to make clay galaxies or do a play. I'll bet we'd even get our picture in the paper."

"Maybe even in books," said Molly.

"Can't you just see Roger's face when our rocket takes off?" said Mary Beth.

That was all Molly needed to convince her. "Let's do it!" she said. "Let's build a rocket and surprise everyone. It'll be top secret. We won't say a word to anyone, okay?"

A shiver went down Molly's back, and she got goose bumps up and down her arms.

"Okay," said Mary Beth. "It's a deal. No one will know but you and me. Unless maybe we need some help."

Molly nodded. "But we won't," she said. She was very anxious to get started.

"Where should we build it? It has to be a place where no one can see it," said Mary Beth.

The girls thought about it.

"In your garage?" asked Molly.

Mary Beth shook her head. "There's no room with two cars. And besides, my mom and dad go in there every day. How about your basement?"

"My mom washes clothes down there," said Molly. "But maybe in the storeroom. No one goes in there till my dad gets out the lawn furniture in summer. Will we be done with the rocket before then?"

"We have to be," said Mary Beth. "We

only have three weeks to earn our badges. And the camp is this summer. This is only January. We'll have to be on the moon in less than three weeks."

The girls ran into the Duff's house and down the basement steps. They pulled open the door of the storage room and looked in.

"It isn't very big," said Mary Beth.

"We'll make a small rocket," said Molly. "Just big enough for two. You and me. And some Tang and astronaut food."

The girls ran upstairs.

Mrs. Peters had gone home, and Molly's mother was reading the paper and drinking a cup of tea.

"Can Mary Beth and I use the storeroom in the basement for something private?" asked Molly.

Her mother looked suspicious. "Is it for something dangerous?" she asked.

Both girls shook their heads. "No," said Molly. "It's not dangerous."

"All right," said Mrs. Duff. "If you promise to clean up when you're finished."

"We will," said Mary Beth.

The girls thanked Molly's mother and dashed downstairs to make plans.

They unfolded two dusty lawn chairs and sat down. Then Mary Beth said, "How do we start? Don't we need some kind of directions?"

"I've never seen directions for making rockets," said Molly thoughtfully. "I mean, there are no patterns or models, are there?"

"I don't think so," said Mary Beth. "I've never seen them in those pattern books, or at the hobby shop."

"I guess we're on our own," said Molly. "Mrs. Peters said we are creative. And I have a good imagination, you know."

Molly left out the word *wild*, which was

how her parents often described her very active imagination.

"It seems to me that all we need is some wood and nails."

"There's lots of old wood in my garage," said Mary Beth. "I'll bring it over tomorrow."

"And my dad won't care if we use some of his nails," said Molly.

"Okay, I'll see you tomorrow, then," said Mary Beth.

Molly waved to Mary Beth and went up to her room. She wondered if she had bitten off more than she could chew.

If it worked, they would prove to Roger once and for all that girls could do anything just as well as boys.

But if it didn't . . . Well, Molly would cross that bridge if she came to it.

CHAPTER 4

Rocket Fever

The next day after school Mary Beth came over with lots of boards. She and Molly tried to get them downstairs quietly so that there would be no questions asked.

"I found a book in the library with pictures of rockets," said Mary Beth. "I thought we could look at the pictures and try to make ours look like them."

The girls looked at the book.

"Ours won't be that fancy," said Mary Beth. "Or that big."

"Or have so much metal," frowned Molly. "But who cares?"

She took some of the wood pieces and laid them side by side on the floor.

"Let's nail these together," she said. "I think that's the best way to begin."

Molly laid some wood in place and Mary Beth nailed. Then Mary Beth put the wood down and Molly nailed. Some of the nails bent in half. Some flew across the room instead of going into the wood.

"These nails aren't very sharp," said Mary Beth.

"Maybe we should use tape," said Molly. There was some black tape on her dad's workbench.

"This is much better!" said Mary Beth, wrapping long strips of the tape around the narrow boards. "When we get them all taped together, we'll bend it to make it round like a rocket!"

"We'll need windows," said Molly.

"That's too hard," said Mary Beth. "We can't have windows."

"How can we see?" asked Molly. "It will be dark inside the rocket."

"Flashlights," said Mary Beth.

That made sense.

The girls taped and taped. They stopped for lunch, and then they taped some more. The rocket was getting bigger, and when the girls bent it, it was a little bit round. Molly found a pole from the yard umbrella to hold it up. It didn't look very steady.

"Boy, the time sure goes fast when you build a rocket," said Molly. "We've been down here all day long!"

"But look at all we've done!" said Mary Beth, pointing.

Molly looked at the taped-together boards. They didn't look like the rocket in the picture. They looked like boards with Band-aids on them.

But it was a rocket. She knew it and Mary Beth knew it. And when they got their space

food ready and started for the moon, *every-one* would know it!

"I'd better go home," said Mary Beth. "I'll come back over the weekend."

Molly felt dirty and tired. She went upstairs and took a bath before supper. When she came down, her dad was home from work.

He looked over his glasses at her. "Is everything all right down there in the dungeon?" he asked, smiling.

Molly nodded.

"Did you do your homework?" he asked.

Molly was shocked. She had been so busy building the rocket she had forgotten all about homework!

"I forgot," she said. "I'll do it after we eat."

Molly felt nice and cozy in her pajamas and robe eating dinner with her family. Was she sure she wanted to leave them and go to the moon? Of course, she would come right back. They didn't have to stay there long, she thought. But what if there was trouble in space?

She decided not to think about that now. The important thing was to get a badge and show Roger that girls were as smart as boys. And of course to win the trip to Camp Blast Off.

Molly wanted to crawl into her bed and read a book that was not about space. But she couldn't. She had to do her homework.

That night Molly tossed and turned and dreamed that the rocket with no windows went up into space without them. Mrs. Peters said, "No badge," because there was no rocket. Would that really happen after all their hard work?

CHAPTER 5

Chocolate Moons and the Milky Way

That weekend the girls put two boxes in the rocket for them to sit on. They put a loaf of bread and some candy bars and a flashlight in too. They tried to tape some wings on the rocket, but they fell off.

"Spaceships don't have wings anyway," said Mary Beth. "We don't need them. It's not like an airplane."

On Tuesday they had their Pee Wee Scouts meeting. Everyone was glad to be back at the Peterses' house again.

After talking about good deeds, Mrs. Pe-

33

ters said, "I have good news. Next Tuesday we're going to the planetarium."

The Pee Wees shouted and whistled.

"I think it will give us a good feeling about space," said Mrs. Peters. "Being there is like being surrounded by the stars and planets. Today I want to talk a little more about space. Then we'll have a little treat and hear about how you're coming along with your projects."

The Pee Wees cheered again.

"As you know," said Mrs. Peters, "space is all around us. And far out in space are the stars and planets. Who can tell me the name of a planet?"

Hands waved.

"Asparagus," said Sonny. "And petunias."

Mrs. Peters looked baffled. So did the other Pee Wees.

"Mrs. Peters," said Rachel, "Sonny thought you said *plants*."

Mrs. Peters smiled. She wrote *planet* on a big piece of paper. Then she wrote *plant*.

"A planet is a heavenly body," she said. "And a plant is something that grows in the ground."

"I thought angels were heavenly bodies!" cried Tim.

Rachel rolled her eyes and sighed. Mrs. Peters explained the difference between angels and planets.

"I will name a planet," she said, to avoid any more confusion. "The planet we live on is called Earth."

"But we aren't in space," said Tracy. "We're right here. The stars are out there."

"We're in space too," said Mrs. Peters. "But it doesn't feel like it. If we were on the moon or another planet, we would be able to see the earth through a telescope."

The Pee Wees looked confused. Space was not easy.

"My dad has a big telescope," said Jody. "Sometime we could all go to my house and use it."

"Great," said Mrs. Peters. "We'd like that. Now, some of the other planets are Mars and Jupiter and Pluto. There are nine planets in our solar system. Jupiter is the largest. Pluto is the smallest. And there may be many other solar systems in our Milky Way."

"How come they have candy bars way out there?" asked Roger. "Who delivers them?"

Mrs. Peters smiled. "This Milky Way is not a candy bar," she said. "It's one of the galaxies in the universe. Our galaxy."

Mrs. Peters held up pictures of the Milky Way, and of each planet, from the biggest to the smallest. "The sun is a star. It's larger than all the planets put together," she said. "The planets revolve around the sun. As the earth spins, the side we live on faces the sun, and we have daylight. Then our side of the earth turns away from the sun, and we have night."

Suddenly Tim began to cry. "I don't want to spin around. I'm going to fall off!" he sobbed.

"I'm dizzy," cried Sonny, holding his head in his hands.

Mrs. Peters held up her hand. "No one is going to fall off," she said. "Gravity holds everything on the ground."

"Everyone knows that," said Rachel in disgust.

"There isn't much gravity in space," said their leader. "That's why it's so hard to walk on the moon. And why the astronauts float around inside the space capsule."

"My mom says you don't weigh anything in space," said Kenny.

"How could you not weigh anything?" asked Lisa. "If you didn't weigh anything,

you'd be a little tiny crumb like Alice in Wonderland! You know, after she drinks from that bottle that makes her shrink."

"Perhaps that's enough to remember for one day," said Mrs. Peters. "Let's have our treat and hear what kinds of projects all of you are working on to earn your badge."

Sonny forgot about being dizzy from spinning around so fast. He grabbed the plate of cupcakes from his mother, who was assistant Scout leader and always brought the treat. Today the treat was in the shape of chocolate moons.

"Space cupcakes!" shouted Roger, gobbling one up in one bite. "Hey, look, I ate the moon!"

After the treat, everyone raised their hands to tell about their projects.

"I'm making the planets out of lightbulbs," said Tim. "I know that will win the contest."

"He makes *everything* out of lightbulbs,"

said Tracy. "Every single project of his has lightbulbs."

"How can he make the planets out of lightbulbs, Mrs. Peters?" asked Lisa. "Lightbulbs are all the same size, and the planets aren't."

"They are not," said Tim. "I've got floodlights and little teeny flashlight bulbs. The little one is going to be Pluto."

"Good for you, Tim!" said their leader. "You know the sizes already. It was a very good idea to use lightbulbs in your project!"

"I'm using lightbulbs too," said Roger.

"So am I," said Sonny. "I've got a giant one for Jupiter."

Mrs. Peters looked pleased that her Scouts were learning so much so fast.

"I'm writing a report on our solar system," said Jody. "My dad got me this great big book of planets. I can see some of them from our front porch when it's dark. So far I've seen Venus and Jupiter."

"I'm making a galaxy out of milk cartons," said Kenny.

"Milk cartons are square," said Mary Beth. "Planets are round."

"Not all of them," said Kenny. "They have flat parts too. And stars are not round. You'll see."

"We're going to have the best project of all," whispered Mary Beth to Molly. "None of these are as good as a rocket."

Roger overheard her. "Nothing a girl does can be as good as mine," he said. "Just wait and see. It won't be a girl who'll win this contest."

"I hope he's not right," whispered Molly into Mary Beth's ear. If their rocket worked, they would have the best project. But if it failed, they would have the worst. And then Roger would gloat. Molly hated it when Roger gloated!

CHAPTER 6

Dead Batteries

The next day after school the girls worked on their rocket.

"I think we're almost ready to launch it," said Mary Beth.

Molly nodded. They had used up all the boards they had. And all the tape.

The girls got into the rocket. They sat on the boxes. Nothing happened.

"How do we make it go?" asked Mary Beth.

"Rat's knees!" said Molly. "We forgot about the engine! How can we move without an engine?"

Mary Beth had to admit that rockets needed power to move.

"I guess we were so busy making it, we forgot." She sighed. "We might have to just pretend to go to the moon."

Molly shook her head. "That's not the same. Pretending won't get us a badge or win the contest. Maybe we need to get outside help. From some rocket expert."

"Experts cost money," said Mary Beth. "Anyway, there are no rocket experts in Minnesota. We'll just have to put our heads together and think."

The girls sat in the rocket and thought. Suddenly Mary Beth remembered something. She stood up so fast, her box fell over.

"I know where we can get an engine!" she said. "Well, at least a motor. A motor is an engine, isn't it?"

Molly nodded. This was no time to nitpick.

"Where is it?" asked Molly.

"It's at home," said Mary Beth. "My little brother has this toy robot, but it broke. He's still got the insides. They still work. I'll bet it's just what we need!

Mary Beth flew up the steps, and in ten minutes she was back. She held up a piece of metal with a switch on it.

"Where do we put it?" Molly asked.

Mary Beth climbed into the rocket. "I think it should be up here in the front," she said, tucking it under a piece of black tape. "This will be our control panel. Are you ready to go?"

"We can't just go without saying good-bye to everyone!" said Molly. "We'll be gone a while if this thing takes off!"

The girls thought about that. Was it possible they wouldn't see their parents again for a long time? Would they have enough food? Would they have enough clothes in case it was cold?

Molly decided she didn't want to think

45

about it anymore, or she might change her mind about going. Then the big surprise for Mrs. Peters and Roger would be ruined.

"We're ready now," said Molly. "Let's just go!"

"Which way is the moon?" asked Mary Beth. "And who's going to drive?"

"You'd better. It's your engine," said Molly. "I think the moon is that way." She pointed toward the basement window.

Mary Beth sat in front of the controls. The controls were a tiny switch on the engine that said On and Off.

"How do we get out of the basement without crashing into the wall?" asked Mary Beth.

"I'll open the window," said Molly. She got a chair, climbed up, and pulled the window open. A cold breeze blew in, and some snow.

"Okay," said Mary Beth. "Say good-bye to the earth!"

Molly's goose bumps were back. Mary Beth put her hand on the switch and pushed it to On.

The girls felt a rush of fresh air, but it was not because they were moving. It was because a stronger breeze was blowing in the window. The rocket stayed where it was.

"Isn't the engine supposed to roar?" asked Molly. "Aren't we supposed to move?"

Mary Beth pushed the switch to Off. Then to On. Then to Off again.

"I know the trouble!" she said. "These batteries are dead!"

She took two batteries out of the motor.

"We can use the flashlight batteries," said Molly.

"Those are too big," said Mary Beth. "These are little ones. I can run home and get some. Then we'll be on our way to the moon!"

Mary Beth came back with the batteries.

They fit! But the girls did not leave for the moon. Instead, Molly's mother called down the basement steps and said it was time for dinner.

"Do you know what?" said Mary Beth. "We should really wait to take off until our Pee Wee meeting, when all the projects are due. That way we can launch our rocket right from Mrs. Peters's house, and everyone will see us."

Of course! What had they been thinking of? It would be much better to take off when all the Pee Wees were there. When Roger could see them! When Mrs. Peters could witness for herself this prizewinning project!

CHAPTER 7

A Star Named Roger

Molly ate supper and then went to her room to count the days until the projects were due. She was glad she and Mary Beth were ready with their fresh batteries.

On Tuesday all the Pee Wees raced to Mrs. Peters's house for the trip to the planetarium. Before they left, they talked about their projects. And they talked about the astronaut who would be coming soon. Mrs. Peters told them what they would see at the planetarium, and how it would encourage them to win the trip to Camp Blast Off.

"Yeah!" shouted Sonny. "I can't wait to win that contest!"

"My dad is getting labels sewn in my underwear so I'll be ready for camp," said Roger.

"You don't wear underwear at astronaut camp, dummy," said Tracy. "You wear space suits."

"Well, you wear underwear under them," said Roger.

"Do not," said Tracy. "Do you, Mrs. Peters?"

"I think that will be a good question to ask our visiting astronaut," said their leader. "We'll learn more about the camp then, and what the winners can expect."

"That's us!" said Sonny. "Roger and me."

"Wait till he sees us take off in our rocket," whispered Mary Beth. "He'll be singing a different tune."

At the planetarium a woman greeted them and explained what they would see.

"You won't see the actual stars and planets," she said. "But these are a very accurate reproduction. It's as if you're closer to the heavens and can see the details."

"Did she say we'll be close to heaven?" Lisa whispered to some of the Pee Wees.

"You have to be dead to go to heaven," said Tracy. "And we aren't dead."

"Do we have to go to heaven, Mrs. Peters?" asked Lisa.

"Pardon me," said Jody, who was the politest of the Pee Wees. "But I think they're confusing *heaven* and *heavens*. One has an *s* on it."

"That's right," said Mrs. Peters. "The heavens are the firmament. Everything in space."

"So heavens aren't heaven," said Kenny.

"And heaven isn't up in the heavens," said Rachel.

"Yes it is," said Sonny. "Heaven is in the sky."

Mrs. Peters held up her hand. Then she put her finger on her lips. "It's time to be quiet and go into the planetarium."

The Pee Wees entered the big round building and saw pictures and displays of the planets and stars. Signs told how far each planet was from the sun, and which stars were the brightest and could be seen with the naked eye.

"What's a naked eye?" roared Roger. "I never saw any eye with clothes on!"

Everyone began laughing at the thought of an eye wearing clothes, and Mrs. Peters had to frown at them again.

"Now, follow me," said their guide.

The Pee Wees did. They went through a big, heavy door and suddenly were standing in total darkness. They were surprised to see the bright stars overhead.

"Wow!" said Kevin. "This is like being up at the lake at night! The sky is full of stars!"

"But these aren't real," said Tim.

"But you can see more than you could at the lake," said Rachel. "Look, there are Neptune and Pluto—they're so far away we can't see them from Earth!"

"That's right," said the guide. "And there is Uranus, another faraway planet."

The Pee Wees gazed in amazement at the universe.

"It feels like we're all alone in the middle of the sky!" said Mary Beth.

"Like we're wrapped up with stars!" said Rachel. "That's neat."

"Hey, there's the Big Dipper," said Tim. "I know that one. My mom showed me it from our front porch."

"And that's Orion," said Jody, pointing. "The hunter. I recognize the three bright stars in his belt."

"How come there are rings around Saturn?" asked Tim.

"Those are pieces of rock and ice," said the guide.

"The earth is too little," said Sonny. "They got it wrong. We live on a great big planet."

"Many planets are bigger than Earth," said the guide. "Earth seems big to us because we live here."

"Hey, look at the man in the moon!" said Roger. "He really has got a face."

"It looks like a face," said the guide, "but it's really a lot of dark rocks casting shadows and fooling us."

"Those stars are really hot," said Kenny. "I saw a TV program where stars burned a bunch of guys up. There are trillions of them, all fiery and hot."

"I saw a TV program where you can have a star named after you," said Kevin. "You have to pay a lot of money and you get this certificate that says it's yours."

"Is that true, Mrs. Peters?" asked Lisa.

"I think so," said their leader.

"I'd like to own a star!" said Sonny.

Soon all the Pee Wees wanted to buy stars and have them named after them.

"See that real bright one up there?" said Roger. "That's probably named Roger."

"A star named Roger?" scoffed Rachel. "No way. A star named Rachel would sound better."

The Pee Wees would have argued more, but it was so dark that they couldn't see each other to fight. And they couldn't see Mrs. Peters holding up her hand, but they knew she was. Even in the dark.

Pretty soon the guide said the tour was over. The Pee Wees thanked her and poured out into the bright sunlight of the parking lot.

On the way home, they stopped at a place called the Stardust Drive-In. Mrs. Peters ordered all the Pee Wees an ice cream bar called a Chocolate Meteor.

"Hey," said Roger. "I'm eating a heavenly body!"

"We're eating comet dust!" said Jody. "That's what meteors are. If these were real they'd burn a hole in your stomach!"

"Well, they aren't real, thank goodness," said their leader. "They're just chocolate ice cream. But they're a good ending to a day at the planetarium."

CHAPTER 8

Project Liftoff

"Tomorrow the projects are due," said Mary Beth to Molly at school on Monday. "We have to get our rocket over to Mrs. Peters's house."

"I think we should get up early and take it over in the morning," said Molly. "If we wait until the meeting, everyone will see us."

"But they'll see the rocket when they get there anyway," said Mary Beth.

Molly shook her head. "We'll put it in the backyard behind a tree," she said. "We won't carry it down to her basement. Then

59

when it's our turn, we'll go out there and lift off."

"We'll have to be the last project," said Mary Beth. "I'll come to your house before school, and we'll take it over."

Molly told her parents she had to get up earlier than usual on Tuesday morning because their project was due. "And then we won't need the storeroom anymore," she said.

"I can't wait to see what you girls have been up to," said her dad. "Were you building an ocean liner down there?"

Molly shivered when she heard his words. He was very close to the truth.

In the morning the girls got dressed for space, wearing an extra sweater in case it was cold. The rocket might be drafty.

When Mary Beth arrived, they went downstairs and tried to be quiet lugging the rocket up the stairs. It was a tight squeeze through the doors and out into the yard. Some of the boards fell off on the way.

Finally they loaded it onto Mary Beth's wagon and pulled it over to Mrs. Peters's house. They quietly unloaded it behind some trees in the backyard.

"This might be the most important day of our lives," said Mary Beth.

"I thought that was supposed to be our graduation or wedding day or something," said Molly.

Mary Beth shook her head. "This is," she said.

The girls set off for school. While they were there, it began to snow. All day long it snowed. At noon Molly said to Mary Beth, "Our rocket is going to be buried!"

"We can dig it out and brush it off," said Mary Beth sensibly. "My mom does that with the car all the time."

In the afternoon the snow changed to

rain. By the time school was out, the rain had frozen to ice.

The girls slipped and slid to the meeting. "This is bad weather for liftoff," said Molly.

"Pooh," said Mary Beth. "Rockets go through ice like nothing. They have more power than a car."

Lots of Pee Wees were slipping and sliding up Mrs. Peters's walk with boxes and bags and folders and bundles. Some of the projects were big. Some were small. But each Pee Wee was sure that his or hers was the best of all.

"Today is the day!" said Mrs. Peters, opening the door. "Come right in!"

"It is the day!" said Tim, carrying something that rattled like glass jars. "It's a great day!"

"What's so great about the day you bring in another boring lightbulb project?" asked Rachel. "You'd think you were going to the moon, the big deal you make of it."

Molly got more goose bumps on her arms when she heard Rachel's words. Rachel had the project right—just the person was wrong!

There were lots of reports and drawings. Kenny had his milk carton galaxy, and everyone examined it.

"This is a very good model!" said Mrs. Peters. "Very detailed and accurate."

"Wait until she sees mine," boasted Roger.

Patty and Lisa gave a space play. It was very short, and they didn't have costumes. Lisa forgot three lines. Mrs. Peters seemed to like the play.

"Definitely small potatoes," said Mary Beth. "We don't have to worry about them winning the contest."

"They should have at least had costumes," said Molly.

Rachel had brought homemade peanut butter space food, and some moon rocks that came from the museum gift shop.

"How do we know those rocks aren't from your driveway?" asked Sonny. "They don't look like moon rocks to me."

Molly and Mary Beth were thinking the same thing. "We'll find out soon enough if they're real, won't we?" said Mary Beth to Molly.

Molly nodded. When they got to the moon, they could check to see if Rachel's rocks were genuine. And they could bring back piles of their own rocks that would really be real!

"These are not from my driveway!" said Rachel, stamping her foot and getting red in the face. "Our driveway is paved!"

"That is a well-thought-out project, Rachel, and it took lots of work," said Mrs. Peters.

Tim displayed his lightbulbs, big ones and little ones and painted ones. Some had cardboard rings around them, which Mrs. Peters said was very creative.

Roger and Sonny had lightbulbs too. The tiny bulbs were comets and meteors and little stars. Some even lit up! The giant one was painted yellow like the sun.

There was no doubt about it, these projects were good. Jody had written such a long report that it had a cover and pages and pictures and looked like a real book. Mrs. Peters held it up and said that not even someone in high school could do such a fine report. "Maybe someday Jody will be a scientist and publish a real book," she said.

"His project is good enough to win," said Rachel. "And I wouldn't even mind. He deserves to win."

Everyone seemed to feel that way. No one would mind if Jody won, thought Molly. He had worked harder than anyone. Writing the report was probably even harder than building a rocket.

Mrs. Peters looked around. "I think we've

seen all the projects now except for Molly and Mary Beth's."

"Ours is outside," said Molly.

Everyone looked surprised. "Follow us," said Mary Beth.

The Pee Wees put their jackets and snow boots on.

"What in the world can this be?" said Mrs. Peters.

"It's a surprise," said Molly.

The Pee Wees tramped out to the back-yard. Mary Beth brushed the snow off the rocket with her mitten and said, "Molly and me built a real rocket."

"Molly and I," said Rachel.

Rachel should be cheering for us, thought Molly crossly, instead of correcting our English!

But none of the Pee Wees were cheering. They were just staring. So was Mrs. Peters. Staring and shivering.

"A rocket?" said Roger. "It looks like a pile of old boards to me."

"You'll see," said Molly. "Soon we'll be on our way to the moon."

No one cheered. It seemed to Molly there should be a bigger send-off. They should at least wave and say good-bye. But no one did.

"Everyone buckled up?" called Mary Beth.

There were only the two of them, thought Molly. And there were no seat belts. But she shouted, "Yes!" to the pilot.

"All aboard then," Mary Beth called. "Everyone stand back!"

No one stood back. Roger stood right in front of the rocket.

Molly leaned out and called, "You could get hurt, Roger. You'd better get out of the way."

"Yeah, yeah, sure," he said. "I'm really scared!" He pretended to shake all over.

"Geronimo!" shouted Mary Beth, and pushed the switch to On.

This time, Molly was glad to see, something happened! The engine roared! Well, at least it purred. Or buzzed a little bit. It was definitely working. All systems were go.

"Listen to that!" cried Mary Beth. "I knew it was the batteries! We're out of here!"

But they weren't. The engine worked, but the rocket did not move. They were still in Mrs. Peters's backyard, under the apple tree.

"Give us a push," called Mary Beth to the Pee Wees. "We need a little help."

But the Pee Wees were laughing now. Even Mrs. Peters was trying not to smile, Molly noticed.

"Rat's knees!" cried Molly. "Just when the engine got fixed."

"It's not the engine," said Mary Beth, climbing out to look. "We're stuck in the ice."

Molly and Mary Beth gave the rocket a few good tugs, but it was frozen fast.

"I have an announcement to make," said Mary Beth bravely. "Due to bad weather, our launch will have to be delayed. We will launch it when the ice melts. In spring."

"These things happen all the time with real rockets," said Mrs. Peters kindly.

Was she implying that theirs was not a real rocket? thought Molly.

The girls were embarrassed. It had been a lot of work. And now it was a failure.

"I think you girls were very creative to think of building a rocket," said Mrs. Peters. "And you surely deserve a badge for all your hard work. But even in good weather, we have to leave the real rocket launching to the experts."

The Pee Wees filed back into the house, two of them in disgrace.

Roger and Sonny were hooting and laughing at Molly and Mary Beth. But Jody and Rachel were saying nice words, like "Better luck next time," and "You guys really did something different for your project."

"I thought we'd be in outer space by now," grumbled Mary Beth. "I told my mom I wouldn't be home for supper."

It looked as if they'd both be home for supper—for a long time to come.

CHAPTER 9

Let's Pretend

"**I** told you, girls can't do space stuff," snorted Roger when they got inside.

"You just wait," said Mary Beth. "You'll see us launch our rocket in spring when it's nice out."

Easter would be a good time, thought Molly. A good time to prove Roger wrong.

"Roger is going to eat his words," said Mary Beth. "That's what my grandma says when someone brags and then is wrong."

Mrs. Peters started to say something to the group about experts, but then she stopped.

"I don't think she believes us either," said Mary Beth. "She doesn't think our rocket is good enough."

Would Mrs. Peters eat her words too, wondered Molly?

Mrs. Stone came down the steps with a tray of spaceman cookies. The astronaut's helmet and backpack were outlined with blue icing. His boots tasted like licorice.

Molly found it hard to be interested in cookies. They were supposed to be on the moon right now. This was supposed to be the biggest day of their lives.

Mrs. Peters clapped her hands. "Since all our projects are completed, and you all did such a good job, I think we'll give out the badges today. Next week our visiting astronaut will be here, and so will the judge of our contest. Afterward we'll be having a little party to wind up our space study. Jody has kindly invited us all to his house for this, and his dad will let us look through his telescope. Next Tuesday will be a very big and busy day!"

"Yay!" shouted all the Pee Wees. They shouted partly because the badges were coming, and partly because next week there would be even more excitement.

"What does she mean, all the projects are completed?" asked Mary Beth. "Ours isn't."

"It will be soon," said Molly. "But we'd better get our badges today anyway. In case our batteries go dead again or something."

"But we can't take a badge for something we didn't do," said Mary Beth. "Mrs. Peters thinks we made a model rocket, not a real one."

Mrs. Peters was calling out names. Each Pee Wee took his or her new red badge in the shape of a spaceship. When Molly and Mary Beth got theirs, Roger booed them and pointed his thumbs down.

Instead of the best project, it looked as if the rocket was the worst.

On the way home Roger said, "Hey, you guys better get that pile of junk out of Mrs. Peters's backyard."

"It's not junk," said Mary Beth. "Just wait, you'll see."

"Ho ho, in a jillion years we won't see!" said Roger.

When Molly got home, her mother's first words were "How did your project go? Can we see it now?"

There was nothing to do but admit what had happened. When Molly's dad got home, she told both parents the whole story. Even though it was a sad story, she noticed that her parents had to try not to smile.

"It's just delayed," said Molly. "Until spring."

Her dad pulled Molly onto his lap. He said, "Molly, not everyone can build a rocket. Not everyone can go to the moon. It's not that easy. You had fun building it, and that was enough. Sometimes it's easy to mix up what is real and what isn't, you know. Building a model rocket is real. Going to the moon is make-believe. It's like playing the game Let's Pretend."

Molly wanted to cry. But she didn't. Because deep down she knew her dad was right.

"But I'll have to tell Mary Beth we aren't going to the moon in the spring," she said.

Her dad shook his head. "I think she already knows," he said. "She wanted to believe it too because it was so exciting. But I think she'll forget about it before long. So will everyone else."

Rat's knees, her dad was right again. The next day at school the subject of rockets never came up.

CHAPTER 10

Roger Eats His Words

It was easy to forget about the rocket, because everyone knew the big day was coming. The big astronaut–party–contest winner day. And at last it arrived.

After school on Tuesday Jody's dad was waiting for the Pee Wees in a big, long car. It was a car that was made for Jody's wheelchair. The back platform went up and down with his chair on it. Mr. George let the Pee Wees take turns riding on it.

"I wish I had a wheelchair," said Molly.

All the Pee Wees did. Jody got lots of attention. And everyone always wanted to help him. But of course, as Mrs. Peters pointed out, there were lots of things Jody couldn't do that he would like to, like run. But he never complained. And Molly secretly thought Jody had a more exciting life than the other Pee Wees.

"Boy, we never got a ride to Pee Wee Scouts before," said Roger. "This is neat. I think we should get a ride every week."

When Mr. George drove up to the house, there was a big sign across the front yard saying, WELCOME ASTRONAUT EVANS.

"Is he there yet?" yelled Sonny. "Is he going to wear his space suit? Maybe a spaceship will bring him!"

"I'll bet he's a great big guy," said Roger. "You have to be really strong for that job. I'll bet he lifts weights every day."

The Pee Wees piled out of the car and dashed up to the door. In the kitchen Jody's mom was getting fancy food ready, and Mrs. Peters and Mrs. Stone were helping her. There was another woman in the kitchen too, wearing jeans and putting pickles on a plate.

"Hey, who's the lady?" said Roger. "I hope it's not another substitute Scout leader!"

"Come in, come in!" called Mrs. George. "I only wish it was summer so that we could have the party out in the yard. But we'll just have to make do." She smiled.

Making do was not too hard, thought Molly. Jody's house was very big and very fancy. The kitchen was huge, with lots of tables and chairs and a giant TV. Jody said it was even okay to jump on the furniture! Although there were twelve Pee Wees and five adults in the room, there was plenty of space for everyone.

"Hey, when is that astronaut guy getting

here?" said Roger. "Maybe Mrs. Peters just made that up, and there really is no astronaut."

"Mrs. Peters doesn't make things up," said Mary Beth. "He is so rude," she said to Molly.

When everyone was comfortable and had a can of soda pop to drink, Mrs. Peters said, "Well, this is the day we've all been waiting for. I know you're all anxious to meet our astronaut, so I won't waste any time talking. I'm proud to introduce Astronaut Evans to all of you now."

The Pee Wees looked at the door to see if the man was coming in. But no one came in. Instead, the lady in jeans got up and went to the front of the room. She sat on a kitchen stool and said, "Hi, my name is Connie Evans, and I'm glad to be here. You can call me Connie. I'll be glad to tell you about my experiences as an astronaut, and I'll answer any questions you might have, too."

The Pee Wees were stunned!

"Look at Roger's face," whispered Mary Beth to Molly. "That is the face of someone who is eating his words!"

Sure enough, Roger's eyes were big and his mouth was wide open in surprise. His face was turning beet red. Molly decided that seeing him embarrassed was better than getting her badge or building the rocket, or even winning the contest! Roger had said women couldn't be astronauts, and here was one, alive and real! Roger looked as if he wanted to disappear.

All the Pee Wees clapped and cheered and whistled.

Connie began her talk by saying there were lots of female astronauts, and that a person named Sally Ride had been the first woman in space. Connie told them how she had studied to be an astronaut, and how it felt to be in space. She also described what they ate and talked about how

scary it was sometimes when things mal-
functioned.

"At first I felt a little dizzy and sick to my
stomach in space," she said. "There is no
gravity, and being weightless makes you
float unless you're anchored down. So it
takes a while for your stomach to settle."

Some of the Pee Wees made gagging
noises and pretended to throw up until Mrs.
Peters gave them a warning stare.

After Connie had talked a while, she went
into the other room. When she came back
she was wearing her space suit.

"Wow," said Mary Beth. "I guess we
would need a special suit to travel to the
moon for real."

"Probably," admitted Molly.

When she had her space suit on, Connie's
voice was muffled. She took off her helmet
and said, "This helmet is tinted to protect
our eyes from the sun." Then she showed
them her gloves and backpack.

"In the backpack," she said, "are oxygen and water. Two things we can't be without."

Sonny's hand was waving. "Why can't you just get water from a faucet on the moon? Or ask somebody for a drink?"

The Pee Wees chuckled. "Can anyone answer that question?" said Connie.

Rachel's hand was waving. "There is no water on the moon," she said. "Or any faucet or any person. The moon cannot sustain life as we know it."

She glared at Sonny.

"That's a good answer," said Connie. She set her backpack on the table and took off the top part of the suit. Then she took off the bottom part.

"Yikes!" shouted Tim. "She's going to be naked soon!"

Connie laughed and said, "Not quite. But what I want to show you is an astronaut's underwear. It's part of what makes us so bulky. This long vest is made of plastic

tubes, and the tubes are filled with water. This suit keeps us from getting too warm."

Connie went on to tell the Pee Wees that astronauts spent most of their time practicing for the trip. Before they got into a real ship, they used models of spacecraft to get used to being cramped together in a small space.

"We take along a camera like this, to photograph the moon and other planets. We also have a computer on board, and a reading mirror, color TV cameras, and solar shields. When we leave the spacecraft, we wear earphones and microphones to talk to each other," she said. "Otherwise we couldn't hear anything because sound travels through air and there is no air in space. And of course there's no gravity, so there's nothing to hold us down."

Molly tried to take this all in. It didn't sound as if traveling to the moon was a lot of fun.

"Most planets are impossible to visit," she went on. "On Venus people would be roasted by the heat. And Neptune and Uranus are made of liquids and gases and have no hard surfaces on which to walk."

Jody raised his hand and asked how long Connie had been an astronaut. Sonny asked how much money she made, and his mother hushed him.

"Is there a kit to make a rocket?" asked Tim.

The Pee Wees laughed, but Connie shook her head. "I'm afraid not," she said. "It's a long, hard job. It takes years to build and perfect a spaceship, and very specialized tools. It costs a lot of money to launch a rocket into space. A rocket uses five thousand gallons of fuel just to lift off!"

Molly was realizing that she and Mary Beth had no chance of building a real rocket. They should have known better! If rockets were easy to build, everyone would make one. Knowing the difference between real and pretend was definitely a problem for her sometimes.

Connie showed the Pee Wees all kinds of space foods. Everything was dried and took up little space.

"It looks shriveled up," said Lisa.

"Yuck," said Mary Beth. "I think I'm glad our rocket didn't take off," she confided to Molly.

"Did you ever see any little green Martians in space?" asked Tracy.

Everyone laughed. Connie said she hadn't yet, but anything was possible. "It may well be that there are creatures out there who are much different than we are."

Connie added a few things about Camp Blast Off and what the lucky winners could expect there. "You'll sleep in little cubicles, just like real astronauts do, with a sleeping bag. And you'll have a little toilet that has to be vacuumed out. The Pee Wees made gagging noises again and held their noses. "You'll also have a shower that is very, very narrow. The meals are packaged so that they won't float away or drift, and they're microwaved. It will all be exactly like the real thing. In fact, the equipment *is* the real thing.

"There will be an actual countdown when you pretend to lift off. The roar is very loud, and everything vibrates so that you think it will fall apart. It's an imaginary flight, but it feels just like the real thing.

"Just like in real space, you'll tumble like tennis balls over and over and need to be anchored down. It's all perfect training for learning to be a real astronaut."

Roger had been very quiet so far, but now his hand was up.

"Isn't it better for guys to be astronauts than girls?" he said.

Everyone started to boo Roger.

"I guess that's your answer," laughed Connie.

"Well, it's time to give Connie a break," said Mrs. Peters. "And it's time to eat!"

CHAPTER 11

And the Winner Is . . .

The Pee Wees all thanked Connie and clapped and cheered. Then they followed her to the big table, which was set with real dishes and real silverware instead of plastic. In the middle of the table was a big cake in the shape of a spaceship, and next to it was a big bowl of something that looked like chunks of chalk.

"This," said Connie, pointing to the bowl, "is our treat! Space ice cream!"

"It doesn't melt until it hits your tongue, so we put it out early," said Mrs. George.

The Pee Wees rushed to take turns tasting it. At first Molly could hardly swallow it. It not only looked like chalk, it felt like chalk in her mouth. She rushed for water along with the others, and then it began to melt and taste good.

By the time they finished their treat, the sun had set and it was dark outside. The Pee Wees got to look through Mr. George's telescope.

"I can see Saturn!" said Kevin. "And this time it's the real one!"

The Pee Wees could see lots of stars.

"I think I see Roger," said Tracy. The Pee Wees laughed.

As the Pee Wees looked through the telescope, the doorbell rang.

"It must be the contest judge," said Jody's mom.

It was. The judge's name was Mrs. Higgins. After she had had some coffee and a piece of cake, she spoke to the Pee Wees.

"I've studied all the projects very carefully," she said. "They were all so well done that it was very hard to decide which to choose. I wish I had more prizes and more room at Camp Blast Off."

The Pee Wees couldn't sit still, they were so nervous.

"In the end, though, I had to make a decision. I'm happy to announce that the prize goes to Jody George. His book on the planets was very well done and took a lot of hard work."

Now the Pee Wees cheered again. Even Roger looked pleased for Jody.

"If my lightbulbs couldn't win, I'm glad Jody's book did," said Tim.

Jody thanked the judge and said he looked forward to going to camp and meeting lots of new Scouts. "I wish all you guys could come with me," he said. "But I'll take lots of notes and tell you all about it."

"And before I go," said Mrs. Higgins, "I want to award honorable mention to another project, for the most original idea. Even though these two girls can't go to Camp Blast Off with Jody, they deserve mention for their vivid imaginations! Molly Duff and Mary Beth Kelly come in second for building a very unusual rocket ship."

"Unusual is right!" scoffed Roger.

"Rat's knees!" shouted Molly. What a surprise this was! Instead of being warned about her wild imagination, she was being rewarded for it! Wait until her mom and dad heard this!

Even better, Roger was wrong again! It was true that a boy had won first place. But it was two *girls* who had won a prize for their wild imaginations!

Everyone said good-bye to Connie and the judge. They thanked Mrs. George for the fun party. Then they piled into the George's car to go home.

Rat's knees thought Molly, it was fun to be a Pee Wee Scout with a vivid imagination, a new badge, and a creative friend like Mary Beth!